Whiskey For The Uninitiated

Liethers

ISBN: 978-9948-19-112-4

www.lietherspoetry.tk

DEDICATION

We turn to books
For something better than travel
To act as our time capsules,
Our storytellers,
Our secret keepers.
A mosaic of thoughts,
A passport to bewilderment
And haven for magic.

I send this to the curious,
The lost and the wanderers,
The sceptics and the converts,
The new and rare romantics who
Perceive outside the lines.

CONTENTS

PROLOGUE

Why do we drink?

Inebriation – much like poetry – springs from our desire for escapism. It deepens with excess. Rarely does a good drink offer resolve, but it often displaces the boundaries of imagination.

Poetry, for me, shares this intuition with whiskey. It can be strangely confessional and almost prophetic in the way it amplifies the beauty of ordinary language, giving it reverence and splendour. It liberates us from the limited ways we feel, giving us the awareness that everything in poetry is arbitrary.

I don't know what makes a poem a poem. But the disconnect for me is when the poem becomes mutably impersonal and catered to the ego when it can be an incredibly vulnerable thing. It should be explicit and eternal. For real poetry isn't formulaic and the self isn't very important, there can never be rules because poetry is understanding that rules are subjective. There is nothing else like it.

Poetry should be contrivedly and subjectively outside the lines. If this selection of poems aims to achieve anything, it's to return the reader to childhood, to our uninitiated selves. That state where all of the senses are open to new languages, philosophies, and sounds.

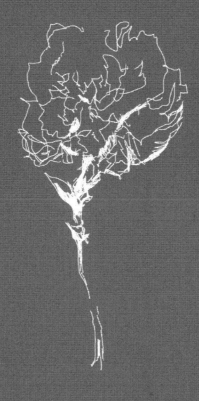

I. Sobriety

"I understood myself only after I destroyed myself. And only in the process of fixing myself, did i know who i truly was."

- Sade Andria Zabala

Happiness is a sunset
Fading behind the shorelines,
Gone for now but not for good.

OPENING OF THE CELLAR TROVE

I found in sobriety
An unconcealing
Of everything that drinking promised but never kept.
I found in art
A healing
Of all the hate that time never cured.

_____

THE SLEEPING

Poetry is a loaded gun
Breathing at us the moment we
Shake sleep from our shiftless heads –
The supple birthplace of dreams
& perfume-born thoughts like
Molten gold wrapped in desire.

Bound in their flat, monotonous orbiting,
The silent sleepers are safe inside a rehearsed ritual
Like a machine convinced of its own consciousness
Most singular and spent,
Untouched by the morning heat
With beached thoughts that could've been lakes
Stranded in the barracks of the mind;
Here a season waits for you.

The sun swells and a fever begins to spread
From the temple to the chest,
A hot muzzle groans
Cherry morning trickles into
the glittering watercourse
Giving the new day its intent.

THE NEW MOON

Fool's journey.
The sunsets of my hometown
Are a dime a dozen.
Leaving home for the first time,
The continents we seek
Seem other-worldly –
Hot to our fingertips,
Like keys hanging unturned,
Dangled in front of our noses,
Scurrying over the vermilion precipice.
Arriving. Setting. Rising.
What far-out splendour ever comes this way?
There's nothing I hate more
Than those which I can't have.
All of our thrills and ruins
Must start and rest in these very playgrounds
As opportunities cycle around us
Unannounced & overlooked.

———————————————

WITHRDRAWAL

Uncertainty is an ungodly mask,
Anxiety leaked through every pore of my body
It's a sinkhole creeping under my feet;
So devoid of all light and chance.
Settled into my discomfort
I shrink in the face of my fears,
They swallow me whole in an instant
Gave me a name for the voices to taunt me by;
The room begins to sway
Ripping me in tatters
Baptism into epilepsy
I turn into a reptile writhing in nylon skin,
So unsure of myself and this torture I've invited inside.
Maybe I'm far too weak for a society that profits
From the fabric of our fears.
These feral beasts lick around my wounds,
These birds of prey hum to the rhythm
Of a drumming in my chest.
Their chants flow in my blood,
My disgraces cuts to the bone
Teeming with yellow neuroticism.
They're coming for me, they'll hunt me down
To tear out all the light left inside of me.

WE, THE PLACEHOLDERS

We hear the lovelorn chapels croon
For the heavy hearts we carry
Not everything is fair in love or war
We're casual foreigners,
Most singular and solitary,
Fleeting in the minds of others,
Warming up beds
Tailor-fitted for new strangers.
I've seen lovers left at the altar,
Fated to fall in love with each other,
Destined not to be together.
Flavours of the terrible summer –
The lorem ipsums of America's sweethearts.
  Ah, the lonely hearts' placeholders.

———————————————

THE DRY DRUNKS

Whether drunk on books or liquor,
Some of us recovering poets will lie;
We'll sell you a dream steeped in rose water,
Sea foam clouds overflowing with gypsy fantasies,
Bottled with our diluted myths,
Corked right after sifting out all wickedness
That have long fermented in their own murk.
A little liquid courage
Mid-morning greys
Incites temperament
To brave a reality where adventures
No longer exist –
Do not fall for this luminary poison.

RUMOURS

The myth of ages
Often omits
The heart-stopping story of our ancestors,
Of how they ignited a facile rumour
(one sweeter than fiction)
A treasure by the waters
Which they called **Love**.

Love left its mark on this world
In the form of ivory hot scars
They say it is immortal
Wearing only the dress its century wore,
The sweetest contempt of generations,
Wounding anyone
Who boasts to have found it.

DREAMCATCHER

It's all coming up roses
Tonight, the city is too busy latching wishes onto
Shooting stars and dreamcatchers
Whose beaded webs bait our wistful invocations.
Refined phantasm perpetually trickles inwards
And leave our sleep entangled
In murmurs of elastic desires.
Our pillows are fluffed with a mother's blessing
Cupping our heads night after night,
Paraphrasing fiction and memory
We hang our heads comfortably low,
Ceremoniously anticipating the day
All our feathered pipedreams to come true,
We almost forgot that nightmares
Are the lesser gradations of dreams too.

SOMETHING BORROWED,
SOMEONE BLUE

Always a bridesmaid, never a bride
She's sat across from me
With her pageant smile in private moonlight
Lying flat under the promenade lanterns and backyard tents
Her love rests heavy and jagged on her palms
With an indentation the shape of an old flame;
But her heart wasn't always this shape…
It was
Borrowed
Broken
Beaten and blue
Before she
Reassembled it from stone.

HONEYMOON

You sit there silently in your heartache.
You must have believed I was magic,
Like the music you imagined when
You were young and spellbound.
The juggling of fire
That excited the blood,
Charmed you to live wilder,
Feel deeper and whisper sweeter.
The warm champagne fizzles out
In the back of our throats
In a sleight of hand,
The butterflies in your stomach
Ceased their fluttering and
The honeymoon daze had set on us
You had so much certainty
Up until that moment.

RUDE AWAKENINGS

Miracles have died in Florence's mind
Making every kinds of silence,
Buried dormant beneath
A head full of memories
She much rather live without.

Unorthodox feet contoured for glass slippers –
Clumsy, inelegant, cold
Behind the backdrop of folklores,
A champagne-haired huntress
Is sweaty palmed from holding on to
Absent hands too eager to let hers go.

Our damsel asks for any excuse
From her everlong distress,
Shaking dreams from her skin,
Itching closer to forgetting love
Just as love
        Forgot about her.

NAKED AS WE CAME

I've seen people dress down to their most honest selves
During sudden fits of rage, spraying their good intentions
Hellishly across the room with such calamitous passion –
It's the only way I've seen others spill their hearts out;
It's the only way we know how.

I've seen generosity hit others like a bullet to the back.
So, forgive me if I'm on edge.
There's something about the stillness of decency
That makes me uncomfortable.
Softness so serene I think I'm going to be sick.
I'm so used to killing others with kindness
And accepting sympathy with a caveat.

———————————————

SEA FOAM LATITUDE

A tide of empathy carries our good intentions
With the softest hands
Pushing back all convictions
At bay until new lens
Offer grand new ways
To see in an age where
The gentle are whipped then eaten.

———————————————

TWO NOCTURNES

Sawubona:
I see you.
I allow myself
To discover your fears, your flaws.
To recognise your sins and accept them.
You are a part of me
And I bring you into being.

Shiboka:
I matter.
Until you see me,
I do not exist.

_____

ILLUMINATIONS

I'm searching for the remnant of dreams
We once shelved,
Swaying wildly
Between patches of false awakenings,
When we smile in our sleep.

The king and queen by the lake –
What ever happened to them?

Did they crystalise
Into stone
In untampered hiding?

Did they wrinkle
From the grisly
Stretch of imagination?

Did they burst into debris,
Exploding the moment
They left our minds?

HUMAN UNBEINGS

The destination is overrated.
Us, flightless skylarks,
We're all in a hurry
To be anywhere but here
In our uncharted slates.
Always chasing uphill,
Under a hum of pressure.
Quite taken by the
Romance of the search
In becoming instead of being.

STELLAR CONNECTIONS

We, the curious,
Are wild hearts chiselled from the same stars
Dangled like jewels, ardently waiting
To be uncovered from darkness.
Gravitating towards each other
In the tidal lock of eternal affinity,
Kindred souls tied together
By an invisible stellar connection.
　　　(soulmates)

A NARCISSIST REPURPOSED

Because I am unloved,
Time in magazines flies like a flightless dove,
Jagged in its uneven semitones.
I'm a self-proclaimed lover, momentarily uncrowned
Dreaming of joys profound,
Intimacy is the flavour of my forbidden fruit
My paradise floats low-hanging and unripe.
How I envied the blind,
    For they've been blessed with a sort of security
How I hated the cypress bark,
    Awakened at dayfall
    Masterfully crafted into a violin;
There's no struggle, no epiphany in their grand design.
Their repurposed selves mock me,
I was spiteful that I could not be them;
They say there's glamour in romance,
And salvation in marriage;
But love is the least menacing of pursuits
And the only thing that gets me out of bed
But if I don't deserve to be loved,
These words are dead in my mouth.

———————————————

II. Euphoria

"We were together. I forget the rest."

- Walt Whitman

Miracles are unpredictable.
Happiness arrives regardless.
Standing in the middle of what could be life,
Happiness heard about you
And in a sudden twist of fate,
Its talons unknotted
In pursuit of you.

———————————————

;

The first kiss
Always takes place
Midsentence;

• • •

And chances are
Your best kiss
Is yet to come.

I could not think of a better reason
To stop a kiss by choice, and leave love
unsaid.

GOLD RUSH

Love, for the uninitiated,
Is in many ways a
Torrential intimacy
Purged from opulent colours
Shone through immeasurable prisms
The gold rush of the 21st century
Gleaming as liquid as the sun;

It is, in all its rare & finite potency,
A spectrum of mutual addiction –
Boundless, all-consuming,
And one of the many amenities of
Drinking.

ENNUI

We are residents of the cellars,
Coddled in the wisdom of the wine
In the mood for new religions
Spilling our hearts with our drinks.
We have willed ourselves into believing
that Liberation exists on stage,
Magic exists in bookshops,
& Love exists in capsuled sanctuaries
Filling a teeming emptiness;
A thirst we refused to call loneliness.

MUTED INHIBITIONS

These harlequin girls flirted with danger
To the same extent our undernourished eyes
Were starved of life.
They adorned their bedsides
With cigarettes, candles
And a banquet of unfriendly strangers.
Black witches consumed by a gospel
That Love is hiding behind unfamiliar faces
Glued to the nearest lips.
Silver streams, crystal starlings
Nimble-footed angels
Smoking coolly,
Trudging rabbit holes
With weighted wings
Lost in the vanity of senses.
Nothing is more forbidding
Than veins injected with liquor
& a head full of troubled thoughts.

UNRETURNED

It's 11:11 somewhere
And I'm all out of souls to sell.
Still folding cheap prayers into paper cranes,
Tossing pennies into dried-up wells
Watching them spiral down in the cloudiest of blues
If any of my postmarked wishes came true,
I was promised one of them should have been you.

AMERICAN BEAUTY

Twentieth-century Americana.
Everything she does is filled with intent
In bold protest against the idea that
Art is supposed to be pretty,
Poetry is supposed to be romantic,
& love is supposed to be easy
For them to be admired instead of tolerated.

———————————————

MISE EN PLACE

We follow the coincidences –
French-suited deck
A shuffle of synchronicities
Our urban routines secret in flow,
Slicing through moments
Dealt to us in a sleight of hand.
Star-crossed revellers
From random walks of life
Two in a billion,
Once in six lifetimes,
Rode up into a gamble,
Like poker players in the dive
Wearing the luck of the draw
While red devils rolled us like loaded dice.
Man plans and God laughs,
Fracturing our will
But here we are: we breathe, we choke
Taking our cues where and who we're supposed to be
At this very moment, at the centerstage of fates.

———————————————————

BLUE HEAVEN

You are a wilderness made of seasons
Dressed in three names during cycles –
You were *No One* in a church to me in November,
Then a *Prayer* to my lips by December
And *a slice of Heaven* to me by January.

THE DIVE BARS

We're languidly wafting kisses to strangers
In the serpent-like alleys of foreign cities,
This is a good place to fall in love as any,
Unwarily abandoning a thousand half-passions
Until we meet someone to love.

STUPEFY

Infatuation wrung our brains of their eloquence
And dried our tongues of all their speech
Until we're so dumbfounded by
All its intangible magic
That we forgot which language to kiss in.

WICKER MAN

Ember eyes on fire
Whiskey hot tears drip down,
Burning my cheeks
Kerosene desire sticks,
It sets my throat ablaze
Inside I'm burning.
I am in flames. I am in love.
And only excess can extinguish me.

———————————————

JAMAIS VU

Can we reminisce on a love
We've never known?

Miss the tenderness in kisses
Never given away?

Long for the warmth of hands
We've never held?

Drown in vacuous champagne eyes
Who may never meet ours?

Suffer from a sort of someone-sickness
For strangers without names?

———————————————

SYNAESTHESIA

Look out for art in the most unlikely places.
Cathedral rose windows refract
Overtones and colours within
The blended auroras of Synaesthesia –

The sanguine rouge of a mother's cry,
The golden earthiness in polished jazz.

The opaline ballet of tides against shorelines,
The fleck of lemon verbena in infant laughter.

The rusty stench in the throes of anger,
The soft and velvety honey in the syllables of your name.

Colours that only revealed themselves when you taught me.
Hues that I can't taste with anyone else.
What a shame you can't see how you amplify
Beauty beyond these stained panes,
The centre of all beauty!

TIME IMMEMORIAL

For reasons of the heart…

I have no memory of falling in love,
It must have happened during one of my blackouts.

What I do remember is the spark of sensuous electricity
Between our fingertips when we touched, anxious

Not to let yours go
And the stirring in my gut when I finally did.

The spin cycle days that bled young and nightmarish
Whenever you were gone

And your once strange face
Ever-so-gently feeling like home.

———————————————

FREE POUR

Your name rolls off my tongue
Like God's most sensual poetry
A fraction of infinity
Older and wiser than me
The shameless kiss of its rhyme
Starts so soft and sweet.
Then pulls like the dragging of a fiddle
Across unmade hallowed grounds.
(Magnus Opus)

SILVER LINING

The universe breathes in our deep-seated fears
And exhales a sigh of hope.

———————

The best way to say 'I love you' is often and fervently.
The only way to love is completely and unreservedly.

———————————

HYPOXIA

The glacial dog days are finally over,
The sun will shine not on us but in us.
We will reclaim the skies.
Somewhere the breeze will be kind,
And fill our lungs with new beginnings.

Take back the new sun, its fever and rage.
A sign of your goddamned times.
Let us go back to the wilderness,
Run wild for our joys, our calm…
Faster for our lungs aching for the taste of air
And new breaths yet to be taken.

A good friend told me,
Sometimes you close your eyes
To remember all that we lost to the flames,
Hold on to your heart
You're safe here, child, you're safe.
Better days have found us.
Hold on tight, chances are
Our best days are on the other side of tomorrow
Waiting for us to wake up and get there.

_____

She is that flavour of perfection that stretches your sensations and makes you doubt reality without so much as a kiss.

———————

MOSAIC

Love's eyes are a sweet Hepburn brown,
With hair that's London grey
Draping over a chardonnay nape
Nourished by marigold kisses.

Her Kathleen Turner cold, haughty sighs
Her sunny Grace Kelly smiles,
Lined with lipstick that's a fearless Swift red
    to spite the day.
Her regal Spencer hands lined by
Midas' touch of canonical beauty
in profuse streams of blue-gold,
Meting out ardour just as handsomely
    as she deserves it.

———————————————

SUMMER SOLSTICE

I have sung of you
Right where we found and lost love
A thousand times refusing death in the garden,
Slipping through the cracks psychically
In tokening re-runs of the same day.
I need another beginning, a different ending.
Our seven minutes in heaven
Are trapped in an hourglass,
Stranded in the longest day of summer
There you were in the heat of limerence
A thousand mornings after
For me to love
All over again,
For what seems to be
The first time.
    What the mind forgets
    In half a breath,
    It takes the heart
    A lifetime.

III. Bewilderment

"It was bewildering, the way reality could be overtaken,
wrestled down, and murdered by the sheer weight of
possibility."

- Jennifer Dubois

TRAINSPOTTING IN MUNICH

Happiness is a train to catch –
Certain but seldom on time
Crowded with searchers and wanderers,
Strangers drifting on platforms, counting trains
Making a wish on each passing coach.

Happiness roars, going ninety miles per hour
Elusive yet still within reach.
Listen to it rumbling on its tracks
It's coming for us, as fast as it can
Eager to carry us home
Taking us from *if* to *when*.

———————

In this secular society, we find miracles in vulnerability, romance in honesty and wisdom in poetry. These are our passports into bewilderment and our most profitable pursuits.

CLOSING GATE PANIC

This is a call to the wanderers,
Your closing-gate panic.
The slender willow-woven highways
Of the coastal silk road,
Off the beaten track,
Stretching to the chances not taken.
Whetting an appetite for
That wisp of white and blue recourse,
The vesper sirens leading our sailors home.
Wherever you are tonight, at exactly this hour,
Take a deep breath,
You're now entering
Someone else's road untraveled.

————————————————

ROAD DAYS

We need friends clothed in
Different cultures of madness
Who teach us art & magic
In sporadic Sunday afternoons.
Rarely have I felt more enamoured
than in Rue Saint-Rustique, casually dressed
And deep in conversation,
The summer of wine, cinema and chain-smoking,
A devouring rush spreads from my heart down to my legs
Arriving at the mouth of the evening
Knocking back shots of Irish cider
As we swim through the sweltering boulevards,
Tottering down the umbilical railways
Veining precipitously towards our
Roaring mischiefs at Père Lachaise,
Skinny dives into the ice-laced Seine
Or revolts at Champs-Élysées.
We need new skeletons for our closets,
We nightmare the slumbering with
One more off key prose from Marseille to Rouen
Chasing down mercurial highways
In pursuit of grander road days
Outside of the ordinary.

———————————————

THE LORDS OF MISRULE

Polaris out of sight! Where are the wise men?
In our golden bricked road, there are no true norths,
Nothing between us and the glowing hill.
We climbed the jewelled rooftops, oh, how they hold us
We chased the light of freedom, arms outstretched
To a burst of feverish ivory
Streaked with purple and green
Flush lantern-burnt nights
Flatter the waving homecoming queens.
Hearts don't break around here
Bourbon-laced miracles sanctioned to embrace us
Liquid luck and madness skirt our calendar laze.
In vain, we hard lads
Find our wild in dances,
Stringing up a crown of beads; our talisman
To scatter around wrought-iron cottages.
The hearts on St. Charles leave no time to regret –
The lesser kings and the sacrifice
Who know of no faith, no penance that will absolve us
For wasting our youth.

LA RÊVEUSE

She was born a dreamer;
Not all over,
But handsomely speckled in deliberate spots.

She daydreams of adventure
Circling the dark continents
Of her mind.

Embarking on every tomorrows &
All the mornings of the world –
Into a wilderness of dreams,
A constant well of pleasures
With a thousand new guises
In the freedom of madness.

Stirring colours in her memory
Rudderless in the lucidity
Extending fingers endlessly.

Inner strife with her clouded vision
From the cataracts of good and evil
Drowning out every voice of reason.

Disintegration
    Of the senses.

SURFEIT

We search for soul in everything –
There was a great serendipity in finding
The others who also found consequence
In the dormancy of an overthought life.

———————————————

FOLIE À DEUX

To be vulnerably honest,
I much prefer to break bread
With a curated band of friends
Over those rare soul connections.
In them, I found a place to rest my head –
    A museum of blackouts,
      Broken into thrillful galleries of
            improvised jazz
      And juvenescent maelstroms by the urns.

I want the sanctity in solidarity,
Feeling wasted in the madness of reverie
And somewhat bored of the frailty of pleasantries.
The heart selects her own society
And grow fond of incredibilities
That quickly turn Friday evenings
Into Sunday afternoons –
Our stories only ever bleed gold
In doses of folie à deux ou plus.

ASTROLABES
(the ones who catch the heavenly bodies)

We are not our worst days
Nor our best;
We are maps charting chances,
Crossing out possibilities
Leading to our hopefully ever afters.

_____

CHIROMANCY

Her finger mapped the creases
On an open palm,
And carved a new fate line
To better suit her Broadway aspirations.

SMALLTALKS ARE FOR LYING, WHISKEY IS FOR TELLING TRUTHS

West Hollywood bungalows,
I'm sick of your small talk.
Drop me a line,
Call me when I'm half-asleep,
And skip the hellos.
Keep the conversation from dropping light.
3am fireside thoughts,
Leather-bound secrets,
A reprieve from LA pigeonholes
Ripped right from the middle of complacency.
Inner sanctums of The Viper Room
It all seems so criminal.
A killer swells with the deafening silence
Tell me about your pageantry blues,
Why you place your trust in a god,
In money, union & gin.
Heartbeats on the Alex Theatre murmur,
Swaying to the populated solitude.
Don't be a stranger,
The City of Lights is in excess
        of lost angels.

NEAR LIFE EXPERIENCE

We are the lost causes, the orphans,
The best minds of our generation.
Larger than life,
Stripped of our names
With only our body count and regrets
Hemmed to our own shadows.

Our lives are measured in ketspoons
We revelled psychically,
Embraced in bated breaths.
In our shared grandiosity,
We ran wild, soared, loved.

We mutinied against a choreographed fate,
In search of something longer than time.
In solidarity, we defy it –
This is our
Near life experience.

Be careful of books.
They unlock everything for us
& make escape artists of us all.
You will find yourself in the painted fog of these pages
Possessed with a lust for someone else's life.

‒‒‒‒

PHANTASMAGORIA

There's a light that never goes out
Slipping out of time
From the heaving of your chest
A gold rush or phantasmagoria
A feverish pursuit of finite sparkles
Lifting your feet off the ground,
Painting the wildest regions of your heart
With vibrant hues of magic and beauty
Incensed, fighting headlong to escape &
Scratching its way out to live fuller.

UNBOUNDED SKYLARKS

She sheds her porcelain skin into gold
And wears her skinned knees
Like the lustrous plumage sloughed off
Lithe silver starlings,
Moulting;
Blowing away with the changing winds
Allowing her to soar higher;
Tired of carrying the remains
Of whom she used to be.

———————————————————

IHSAN (إحسان)

The sun fell into holy waters
An ivory sunburst
Shone golden through absinthe gulfs
With its heart tied
To a vein of stars
Lapping against the impossible dust.

I tugged on their viridescent strings
And spilled a rain of light
An explosion of constellations
Like a tipple of fire and silk
Dappled in glimmers
Across the obsidian sea,
Orbiting histories beneath our feet.
And for a moment,
Inside their ancient wisdom,
We were infinite.

INNOCENCE

From inside a rabbit-hearted girl's rib cages
Loomed an edifice of
Wishbones –
    Galvanised by a dreamy languor
    And all the prayers that her hands can make –
Stationed in place where her spine
Should've been.

When a mad storm
Christened her
It pulled on the prongs –
Snapping them clean in twos,
And walked away
With the bigger halves.

———————————————

IMAGINARIUM

Come to the sea, my love
Come closer and see
Chimeral dreams of comely girls
Channelling little purses of
Cool, otherworldly sensations.

Tasting colours screaming through kaleidoscopes
Savouring synaesthesia with
Wild exuberance. Invisible cities.
Tremors from a light tower
Expanding our visions.

Electric souls writhing inside a pipedream
Where the mind is ash blind.
The mouth fills with the taste of copper
The drunken throat is spitting blood
To tell apart sobriety from a devouring stupor.

It's a shame how I must first lose my youth
For a swill of your bewilderment;
How I lost my compassion
For a taste of your enlightenment.

TO KILL A KILLING LONELINESS –

I found an anaesthetic
I so desperately need
Pretty as a devil, smooth as sin
Wearing star-painted champagne eyes
That put to the shame the Norwegian night skies.
She kills a killing loneliness –
She was airy hope deferred;
Rekindling my romance with regret
& gluttony for a kind of happiness after you.

———————————————

The conversation of prayer

Is a love affair

Between

Magic

Fervour

Energy

& Passion

IV. Stupor

"Every time my stupor turns into vibrancy, standing
around is not an option."

- Saim Cheeda

Happiness is a fickle beast
    who promised us our pound of flesh.
Elusive in poise and endlessly deferred,
Gnawing us open and piecing us back together
In its infinite changes of heart.

Old friend,
We have loved you for the last time.

———————————————

DISCONNECTED

I want life. I want to feel it, read about it, live it. Now is omnipotent, all the rest is remembered. We have wasted so much time traversing inwards, whiling away inside the sandboxes of the mind instead of reality's. Disconnected from the world rather than in sync with our surroundings – never in the moment. There's too many of us running our fingers through the human imagination that we've fetishized so much, exploring unspeakable worlds under the clutch of the bottle. Infatuated with what could be, afraid to come to terms with the world we escaped from.

now is

omnipotent

All the

rest

is

only

remembered.

LETHARGY

She exists inbetween the vicious cycles
Of sleep and superstition
"Alive!" she cried.

———————————————————

Fear & superstition
Are self-perpetuated;
Do not fall
Into believing
Everything
That you think.

FORMING SECOND IMPRESSIONS IN NEW YORK

We abused so much time by
Making up our minds about
Foreign films that put us to sleep,
Indie bands who penned strange, new sounds,
The rubbled temple art at The Beagle,
The bottles of overdiluted soju in a garish bodega,
And the emotionally bankrupt residents of 6 Train.
The cool rain lashes a mirage in a puddle –
Once bitten, twice shy, we're
Slamming the doors shut behind us
Scuffing our cold feet to get around
The trampled metropolitan foliage
Our crooked sundial on the High Line,
Storm-strangled streets we used to run,
A graveyard for a thousand first loves & old selves.
Everyone here is searching for something more
Actresses trading in rose gardens for the Madison
Square,
Broadway marquees trodden by impermanence,
Piano man burning sticks at every dive bar,
Gunshot brides fled the same loveforsaken chapels,
Reverberations of histories relived –
We left a part of our pasts in New York.

WHISKEY DIVINATION

I am an Auror
with a vision of rude awakenings
Looming large over the horizon
 A stormy prophecy;
 A misfortune-reading
Sitting shipwrecked at the
Bottom of my drink.

My own heady brand of
 Whiskey Divination
Lifting the looking glass to my lips,
Swallowing burning needles
Satin inferno trailing down my throat;
Electric tasseomancy
I can tell when I'm in trouble -
I will take my place
Half seas over
Without reservation.

_____

ON THE ROCKS

The maiden voyage
A lost child's paperboat faces the moon
That beckoned it away from the coast,
Mired in the subtle play of light and whitewater,
Capsized into water tombs
Upon emancipation
Unreturning from the overflow
Wandering through the thick of the night
Without seasons or stars.

OBTUNATION

Summer is an open bar
Her nights are long and her regrets are cheap
We are the new breed of romantics
Who slept in last night's clothes and tomorrow's guilt
Charged by a shot of whiskey on one hand
And a jigger of bad judgements straight to the heart
Chased down with a stranger's kiss
That sits upon our lips
Long after our blackouts've bowled over
And mistakes've been made.
I came to in the middle of a bedroom hymn,
A clutter of memories trickles back in
Crowded with lover to lover
With their greed to please and forget us.

———————————————

THOUGHT IMPEDIMENT

Another case of the brain fog –
I came to realise we haven't spoken in years,
Tongues tied behind a muzzle,
An impediment bites my teeth
Embroidering the break of my lips.
How little I thought, how much I felt.
My mind is clogged of authenticity
All perceptions I conceived sincerely
Have turned into sludge
That's lodged itself in the back of my throat.
A thrush of counterfeit thoughts handed down to me
Pricks the roof of my mouth,
Scorching my tongue like a pyre for the right words.
My throat is charred with fear of
The sound of my own voice
Ricocheted back and forth against my jugular
'cause the heart hides such unimaginable things
Trapped between two lungs.
Jaws agape, chagrin seeps through my skin,
Barrel-aged truths rattles behind my lips,
Jagged & out of place –
I was screaming out a language
I never knew existed before
Butchered as they crawl their way out:
        Luminous & combustible,
Only to be whipped back inside
By a forked tongue lashing sardonically
        With dour conformity.

DUPLEXITIES

I inherited my mother's backbone
And my father's cold feet –
      The push and tug of tides –
My feminine voice seeks intimacy
My masculine energy searches for expansion
Contractive nature surrenders to ease and flow
            Unrequited and allowing
A giving ego steals my thunder
            Outward and protective
A tug of war of duplexities
Androgynous temperaments:
She is a part of me
 & he is wounded.
I am absolute.

People have a poverty of imagination when it comes to
finding potential in others.

———————

PIPEDREAMS

Stop a moment
Oh, how you seem so free!
Lucid dreaming
An aperture to esoteric visions
Extension of the overself
Pouring out of ethereal vapours.

Eyes catch fire & swallow the light
Phenomenal jazz, oaky wine
Grazed our fingertips
Effervescent
Lingering soot
Our divine souvenirs
From the inner world.

BEDLAM FUGUE

Do you exist?
Are you somebody's prayer?
How did you love?
What did you die for?

Frozen inside the snowglobe,
Through the looking glass so shiny and new,
I am the lonelier version of you.
Take me away from this hall
Of smoke and mirrors
My reflection talks back
Amorphous and foreign
I look around and cannot find my face
Every version of myself is
Speaking in confessional tongues
A spinning orchestra of cackles
That have long abandoned
The grammar of reality.
While we're here,
Forgive me father
I can barely remember
The colour of sobriety's eyes
Damn the dusk and our blues
They do not deserve to be eternal!
Out of my element,
Into my downward spiral
Contemplating what to do with myself
Once I sober up from this bedlam fugue.

SOMEONE-SICKNESS

They say the same love never comes twice
We arrived a little late to its promise
With a made-up name & a hand-me-down kind of
                              aborted love
That fate threw at us
Sweeping and scant,
Stolen from us
Young and ill-timed.

The universe made a bed for your fast youth
And what could've been diamonds
In the fixed hours of my every yesterdays
So I may forever be reminded
That Loss still floats in perdition:
Unfinished, loose-ended.

I'm tethered to this someone-sickness,
Concerted by wrong turns and missed cues.
Too young to keep good love from going wrong,
too wild to last.
I'll keep you locked in my head,
Until we meet again
I hope to learn by then
Perhaps, we can never break up
With soulmates.

Is it still considered a heartache
When it's your entire body, spirit, and soul
that feel broken?

RELAPSE

Where are the lords' new wines,
Our dark and potent ecstasy?
I left my mind behind cellars
Fermenting inside the corked bottles
Guzzling the blue into red,
Searching for a cure
For my lack of pastel imagination.
Remove me from these
Conjugal revolving doors of
    they love me, not. They love me.
    They love me, not. They love me.
    They love me, not. They love me.
    They love me, not…
I need new poison to pluck me out of all the wrong arms
And into a new spell
I'm most comfortable out of my mind;
Where my wedlock to reason has crumbled.
Let me sleepwalk in an obedient attraction to fate
While whiskey spirits live my life for me
Stoned in an automatic distraction;
An augmented reality simulation.

_____

Even the warmest embrace
can crush willing hearts
with the harshest of hands.

REDACTED

Where are Pan's lost boys?
Wearing kisses on their supple fingers;
Whose coming of age never arrived.

The bad seeds, the invasive thieves
Never to rise from the motherless soils,
Whose sickly weeds enraged cherry blossoms –
Whose flights of fancy were nipped in the bud
Locked to rot in the supple skulls
Of kids who didn't make it.

The jury of twelve has made a bed for them,
The world has never wanted them less.
Time buried their light along with
Their infancy
And witness them sprout fervour
From the ground
Up.

IMPURE

Windswept Parisian courtyards lined with
Sacred sculptures gilded like rainfall
Scattering picturesque light
On aristocratic grounds
Versailles calling –
Oh, how you flood the inebriated brain
Of a weary-eyed stray
With a glint of cinematic images of
The night's wild divinity and the cavalry
Nestled at the heart of sullen streets.
Androgynous High Style
Cleansing the soul of unculturedness
Like blessed liquid light perfuming
The derangement of our senses
Causing the heart to stutter
Surrendering to its rhythmic slurs
(Qu'un sang impur
Abreuve nos sillons).

CLOUDING OF CONSCIOUSNESS

We heal in communities
Kindred connections
Who usher us out of our shells –
The clouding of young solipsism
Awakening new rituals
Internal voyage
And improvising new streams
Of consciousness along the dark.

LAWFUL MAGIC

I speak in tongues fluently
With an English hoarseness in my voice
In my mother tongue I croon with a softness in my prose,
Stammering exuberantly with a Levantine nonchalance,
Slurring the grammar of intimacy when it's all spun out.
Numb to all emotions outside the confines
Of language & imagination
All this wealth of symbols & metaphors, still
Blind to all the prose of colours yet to be seen &
Tatters of pleasures yet to be felt
Idiolects do not offer the words for
All the miracles that exist, scrawled all around us.
We looked up to a cluster of stars
Where a burning vernacular exists, shiny and new
Poised outside of this world
Gently they dripped from the skies and landed into our eyes
Profound spells that conjure the right Extraordinaires
Such lawful magic written in celestial calligraphy.

THE UNIVERSAL MINDS

It is the mind – with all its claws and teeth –
That govern the universe and the one before it.
Gently we stir from torrential slumbers
We did our time inside
This universal consciousness
Rattling behind its bars
Stunted in an experiential purgatory
Rank and file
It catechised us to seek velvet pleasure in
The monotonous confines of other people's minds.
Consigned to the temple
Imprisoned by time
Enslaved by the ego
In an abiding interest of belonging
Conditioned instead of enlightened –
We are closer to being each other than ourselves.

———————————————————

SLURRED SPELLS

Words are potent spells fundamental in creating events, sculpting the narratives of histories, and transforming the listener and speaker in the process. In their flow, they contain the energy to fortify the senses, to amplify or dissemble tenderness, capable of inflicting or alleviating pain, of bringing us to love and out of it. Use them as instruments to influence others into a vivid reality, one free from the ego. They possess the power to start a religion or turn us against one another. Spill purposely.

EXCESS BAGGAGE

Do you think it is at all possible
That when a person dies,
His soul departs into a remnant of a dream,
Through the doors into eternity and nothingness,
Someplace without seasons or proviso,
Taking along with him
His favourite pieces of our universe –
The rites of the *voyager* –
The first of many endings
Slicing open
The constellations, oceans, galaxies
To piece together a gouache kingdom in death
More grandiose than what he was offered in life?

What will you miss of this world?

_____

NORTHERN LIGHTS

From the primordial
Clouds of gas
And celestial dust,
We forged constellations
Into unbounded chaos
Spinning relentlessly
Around the mouth
Of black holes.
Our sailors voyaged
The flitting emerald ghosts
Swirling until they're locked
In a gravitational embrace
A heavenly brilliance.

THE CORONATION OF SPRING

The Holocene has ended
Child universes birth new civilisations
Time is warping and ever-bending
Cosmos collapse, get ripped apart,
Sage elders gathered around,
Will the transient galaxies
Expire
In ice or fire?
Can we escape before entropy
Destroys it all?
No one gets out alive,
They're going to crucify us
One last explosion
Of glowing embers
Bathes the universe in light
A soft diminuendo
Pirouetting into their final rites.

IN STITCHES

In the process of
Weaving paradise
We've sewn each other's eyes shut
To the spectacle of the universe.
Scenes from behind the velvet blindfolds
Embroidered by a streak of false prophets.

———————————————

JEKYLL OR HYDE

I must have confused your softness & rage
For dichotomies
When they were actually
Contradictions.

MONEY FROM HOME

May the cruellest citylights
and thankless metropolitan rituals
never quell our curiosities
to discover and live sweeter
Godspeed and search on,
  Money from home.

GREEN VERTIGO

The lush green tides of vertigo set in
Through absinthe-soaked eyes
I'm a huntsman with a heart of glass again
Stirring the foaming, fogged pools
Of emerald freedom
A thirst for auroras and ripples.
Life seems tenderest at dusk.
There is an awakening that rends the mind,
Dwelling in the stupor-hushed consciousness
A papyrus castle, the frothed & dilapidated moat
Calling us to levitate into dizzying heights
Where hesitation recedes and eccentricity prevails.

A DWINDLING HIGH

We regress to a time
When we were nearly alive:
The year was two thousand and nine –
Your home is still here,
Prayers used to reach God easier from up here.
Stomping on its threshold is a cure to growing older
Fool's gold rented out to the best bidders.
Coney Island fairs where we found magic
Like mischievous poetry in rock & roll
Dollar franks and candied apples
Perfuming the fifty first days of our flannel summers.
A wellspring of highs possessed by the silver past.
A secret hidden down by the pier,
Tucked under bucolic awnings
Of meagre boulangeries and merry-go-rounds,
Basking in the hot infinite potency of
Inviolate and familiar youth.
But, like warm inviting names
Emblazoned on cold crestfallen faces –
These places no longer exist.
We're free to roam anywhere and everywhere
Except for home.

––––––––––––––––––––

THE POET'S OUTFIT

You saw a broken heart
And salvaged its hallow chambers
With the quintessence of
Vibrancy
Desire
Prophecy
Madness
Soul
Sin
& the wisdom of the overself.

PASSPORTS

What's in a name?
How many secrets can it keep?
Carnelian birthstones plucked from divinity;
Shaping tribal allegiances,
Carrying an ancestral wisdom
Tucked in its muddied sleeves.
What's in a name?
How many hearts can it divide?
The roots of segmentation,
An entrenched foraging of connectors,
A stubborn curiosity in our dreams & visions.
A new story of storms and sin emerges,
Aren't we all travellers?
Sharing a deep-seated honour in new histories
Rising w/ fresh intent breathed into them.
What's in a name?
A sentence on my father and his father before him
How many wounds shall it pass down?
An insignia, our bloodline's coat of arms –
Blueprints of a hereditary fate
Promissory notes that you will never be
Far from Home.

xx

BLINDING LIGHT

Witching hour, 12th August.
Ether limerence came shooting down
Stabbing through sanguine skies
In liberal flashes of diamonds
Sharp-feathered light I mistook for a girl
Splattering trails of brisance
Overwhelming astral conversations
The Perseids spiralling inward in prose
Wrought-iron warhead
Planting craters in the snow
Brewing dust storms
Destruction,
      Mutually assured.

To our past selves:

Maybe the stars weren't aligned for us
Perhaps we read them all wrong
In any event, it will never be enough
To rearrange them on our own.

WISH I WERE HERE

I've been a thought more often
Than I have been someone.
Lethargically wandering
    Heliocentric Arabian summers,
    Temperate emerald forests,
    And starry Dutch rivers,
    I placed myself there, staring at my phone
    Because I couldn't be good enough.
I'm a figment of my own imagination
A voyeur drifting unnoticed along the riverbank,
Hiding in daydreams and silver screens,
Abstaining from materiality, sleepwalking past
First loves, rites of passage and heartbreaks.
Postcard greetings from youth:
"Come back to the present,
The past doesn't need you anymore,"
Stirring a baleful numbness off my hair.
If there's a next time,
I'll do better;
Wish I were here.

STELLARCENTRISM

I trace the moonless horizon
Like a watcher
Of the skies
Welcoming new planets & stars
To swim into his ken;
I basked in your familiar glimmer
Burning luminous and tired
Keeping a dangerous distance
from your centrefold.
Your light travels to us
Reverberating from a distant past
That no longer exists;
A stellar corpse orbiting
A fleeting moment
Lonely & frozen in a cosmic purgatory
Fading smug and unapologetically.

———————————————

WISPS OF SMOKE

It's a curious thing –
moving on
every moniker of love splits our souls
into a thousand shards
fragments of naked memories
where remnants of our waning past
collect dust
frozen as they were.

They have stolen
Horcruxes of our selves
Housed by many a new heart;
Pieces of our identity
they carry w/ them
enslaved as memorabilia
long after they've
g o n e .

A seed must first destroy itself
from the inside out
to blossom into wildflowers.

———————

PICTURE IMPERFECT

So this is love.
It seemed rosier in faded postcards
That never feel quite like we want it to look.
We kept our romance a secret –
Renting out red rooms, sensitive of the light;
Trapped in still frames
Waltzing untampered inside
Technicolour timecapsules
Of the roaring twenties
Where time has paused
Never again will there be
Another time like them.
My history is fully yours, a transient centrefold
Anchored in 8mm photographs
Timeless and picture imperfect.
All we were in memories
Will never be taken from us;
This is us at our zenith.
Life hasn't been any worse but
This is as beautiful as it gets.

APOLLO

He was king of the sun
Pulling a light across the skies
With an arrow and a lyre
As the sultry sunrise rages on.

The west winds bowed to his lustre
Everything the light touches
Made her shine like diamonds
Potent with evergreen beauty.

The east winds crooned while his flare
Casting shadows out of her leaded heart
Against the roots of her heel
Defiling the purity of sunlight
Through his devotion to things out of his reach
Like the moon, the past or her.

BERLIN

We're two brothers fluent in distance
Kerosene boots trample on leather gardens,
The cold summer of 1961.
The fumes were live,
We got close and then ran.
Striking a match, leaving with our head hung low
Torching bridges to shine a tremendous blaze
Never looking back;
Light the fuse and get away.

Robed in pride showering us with sparks
Until we miss
Nothing except one another.

_____

V. Coma

"How nice - to feel nothing, and still get full credit for being alive."

- Kurt Vonnegut

Happiness became our religion
Breaking every other faith into shards
It comes crashing w/ a violent roar –
That counterfeit blast of feverish elation
Feels a lot like it's damn near destroying us
Frozen in a hope-forgotten limbo
Trying to make the most of all the ones who stayed
And the least of the ones that got away.

———————————————

an ode to whiskey:

I came to you
for love
I turned to you
for wisdom
I crawled to you
for peace
I call to you
for magic
and you gave me
lust
illumination
prophecies
an awakening
on the house

———————————————

BURNING THE ICE

A brave new day unfolds
Origami papercuts
Who do I want to be when I open my eyes?

I rehearse the future,
Through an old dream,
Choosing the day,
Be all that you envy,
Burning the ice
Stirring our cerebral desires
Connected to all that is
Everything has led to now.

I become loyal to the present
By taking my body out of the past
Somewhere we are forgiven
In our being now-minded.

KINTSUGI

We are vessels made up of space and time,
Dust and stars,
Mirth and invocations,
Glass and blood.

We've been given our scars as souvenirs
From the not-so-distant past;
Cigarette burns and open sores
The leaden trophies we've got in spades
From the bible-black nights we charted.
Stubborn wounds create openings, niches
Billowing burnt flesh
Swelling to help light filter through,
Our boundless magic seeps through our deformities.

X marks the gilded spot
Where the right muses pieced the shards
Of our former selves together with gold,
Illuminating an undeniable charm in our gilded new skin
Born of our blemishes and deficiencies,
Embracing them instead of sweeping them
Under the rug.

I am an alchemist –
I can stop time
I can transfigure silence
& distance into words
Made up of incendiary thoughts
Coiled in our chests
Harrowing. Deep-seated. Unsaid.

———————

PAPER KITES

Let us stay anchored in our cages
Us, flightless skylarks –
Our clipped wings may be nourished
By the anticipation of pursuit
To kill innocence in an instant;
Static levitation
But our brittle paper bones
No longer seek milk.

Comets are the cold, antiquated wishes
Of unsaved damsels and the forsaken
Which never came true.
And heaven knows,
I've fallen in love with dead wishes I no longer need
And what I've chased won't set me free.

ROTGUT

The excess of religion is an unbidden guest
That creeps into a century
That resists to turn twenty-one,
A sharp metronome is slicing
Into a chokehold of repeating words in my head.

My compulsion recites a pretence that all will be well.
A need for symmetry, a plead for reassurance
I grew tired of the long strides
Over cracks on the pavement & broken mirrors;
Miserably defusing the bombs in my head,
A grappling anxiety that believes happiness is
Stranded 7 years in the past.

I'm too tired of petitioning a rumoured wisdom
In small whispers to the wind
To keep harm at bay,
Afraid that saying it out loud
Makes it more real;
Injecting a poison straight to the mind.

I know that I'm in trouble
When a drumming in my chest starts to swell
And a rotting of the gut starts to stir –
Superstition is not concerned
With whom I pray.

TOURIST SEASON

Her heart was a rose garden
Growing honeysuckle down
Her bare feet
Forging sinuous trails
Through Spring
Withering to thorns,
Devoid of light
During the ceremonial visits of Fall
It's tourist season for new love.

Mandala maze, arid forest glades,
A herbarium of scarlet letters slowly decays.
Arboreal cycle, a native horror show
Primordial labyrinth of highs & lows
Geometrical patterns in ebb and flow
Will she ever find her way out of the olive groves?

Strewn petals of light we've exhausted
The winding steps cobbled with
Draping stalks of wisteria
For her feet to walk on with ease
But bashful flowers can't find their place
To grow in its path undiseased.

IS ANYBODY HOME

Long distance relationships can exist
Among those within arm's reach
Comfortably distant in the secular age
Confined under the same roof with love,
In the same partitioned vein as warmth
And in the same room with mothers & fathers.
Under leprous siloes, these boarded-up duplexes,
Quiet isn't always peace.
Empty bedspaces are just as loud and irremediable
When strangers fill homes with radio silence.
This house used to cradle life
Blood runs thickest when it divides us
Pick a side and I'll take the other.
I was screaming at my father,
I blamed him for the times we hardly talked
He measured his regrets by the wrinkles
Sitting on his weathered skin.
We turned on each other like
Ceremonies turn into rituals
Conversations into small talk
Brothers into well-wishers &
Neighbours into voyeurs
For a city without seasons
It sure rains a lot in Damascus
The communal heartbeat has flatlined:
"Do not resuscitate."

FOR VINCENT

A madman drifts among the ether bedlam
Married to madness –
  Sprawling, hazy, full
Spinning rippled storms of
Washed blue & burnt gold
Turpentine sadness
Bleeding beneath the overcast
Unfit for contemporary culture.

Possessed hands paint their way out of sobriety
Slumped in the twists and swirls of undertows
Dappled autumn whirlpools
The sun-drenched wheat fields,
Cypress-punctured moon beams
And wild irises fluttered.

He enters softly into the gorse maelstrom;
Shaping a self-portrait illuminating
The divorce from the world
Of a cosmic outcast.

LAST CALL

(An hour to death)
We mortgaged our souls
Petitioned for one more hour
To perfect our legacies
& live a life a little more loved
Borrowing hours after hours
Until time becomes hallucinatory.

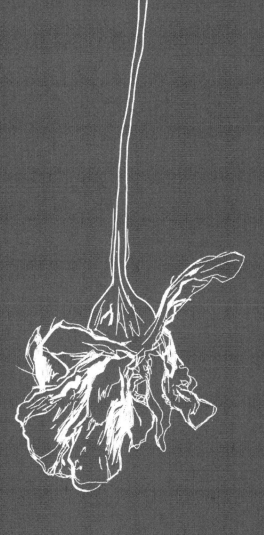

VI. Death

"...we take death to go to a star."

- Vincent Van Gogh

Happiness is like my mother told me –
Rarely ahead
And, often behind us.

_____

We've bottled up
So much of our emotions
I could drink them up now
Whiskey pools of ice
Dipped in a song.
Some nights I taste nostalgia warming my throat.
On others, the bitter aftertaste of livid distress
Picking at the scabs
From the lack of loving memory.

CINE-STHESIA

Death takes centre stage
It's no theatre but it sure attracts a crazed audience
Invoking a sense of comedy to those who worry
A satyr play to those who wait
And tragedy to those who reminisce.

———————————————

LUNE

She was the splendid moon
Two continents will never share
Collecting the hearts of sinners,
Relinquishing herself
To everyone that crossed her path.
Soon, the sun will caress our walls
And she'll gleam her light for someone else
Bowing into a dimming ochre whirl
Wait! I've never been so deathly afraid
Of a new morning to come.

APPOINTED TIME

Time has claimed something from us.
We're journeying into a staged nightmare
Where fascination has come to die.
Time slows down when
Listening to our heartbeats in reverse,
Watching old love
Run its course
In retrograde motion
From the rear-view mirror.

Attraction did not end
At the wake of love;
Nor did love stay dead
When we ran out of all the little gold
    We liked each other for –
They whittled down in dregs the moment
      We ceased discovering
        & celebrating one another.

We left love roughly smothered.
Dressed in black and its prettiest frown,
We paid its body no vigil,
Our pain cannot be reworked.
If only for a night,
I'd give anything to turn this tide
Just as we would wind back a worn-out timepiece.

BOUNDARIES

Nostalgia is an entry wound
It has an element of hollowness to its irresistibility
Rigor mortis spumes, stiffening my joints.
It latches my histories back beside me, open-ended;
I offer no recourse for its mourners.

Enveloped in the mouldy decay of age-old remembrances,
It's a timestamp wrapped in rust
Running laps around
Our laughter and whatever comes after.
Bracketed in wistful ignorance, walled in solid rigidity –
Everything is locked in place
It has no future but itself.
A chain link fences the liminal space splitting between
A time when chasing happiness was the day's religion
To when nothing seemed to please me anymore.

REQUIEM FOR ROME

Citadels rising, the future's sold out
We burnt our pasts at the pyre
The last days of radio,
A colosseum crumbles into mote,
The death of the empire
Washed away by the spring-tide
While we were docked in the safety
Of new harbours enlarging
Spectral nationality
Limitless
Bathing in new mysteries
And the universe's erosion
Perilous and stunning,
Sweltering at the visceral fear
Of change.

Tomorrow belongs to the dreamers –
It waits for the fearless, the daring, the spirited, the bold
Count me out.

———————

INSOMNIA

You could feel
The bloodlines of all
The empires
Free-flowing through her veins,
Pulsating.

She wakes up
In cold sweat,
With her head
Still buried
Inside books
As she loses sleep over all
The lives she hadn't lived.

INCUBATION

In that year, we were estranged
from the concrete wilderness
City noon looted of peace
Behind the frosted hotel glass, we're a cluster of breaths
Laurel blossoms starving for daylight
Grappled into wreaths, a ring of roses
That smelled of the green plague lurking outside.

Incurably alone, disconnected
Inviting death and illness inside
Stranded in a sunless, frozen hell
Our hibernating caves converted into funerary boxes
Veterans of war wrestled into this bated silence
Of radio-dark summers
Peering the morgues through willow eyelets.

Snow-hushed dreams were planted forgetfully
Chalked in the soils of Potter's fields
Slowdancing around graves
Six   isolating
    feet   apart.

LANDFALL

Hitchhiker in anticipation of landfall
My redbone roots
Are you waking up slowly?
Despondently holding your breath
      Waiting quietly to live
The life you deserve
The Western dream
Taunting your flesh,
A tapestry of unworthiness
Purpose-thieved hands wounded by
Melanin landmines.

REDOLENCE

Perfumes – the only art of time travel known to man. Our memories and emotions assimilate themselves to scents, giving them a handwritten identity, indiscriminate of the illegible stories they bottle. Sometimes, it's the cool fragrance in the splash of earl grey that transports us back in the arms of a mother, nuzzled upon the safety of her breasts. Other times, they carry no elegance in the green danger looming underneath a paraffin-scented musk. Their fumes fill the room, reminding us of how certain words have now become forbidden to our senses, like curses or a name trespassing from our past. Afraid that uttering them will invite the harm back into our present lives.

ROADKILL

Frozen still in the headlights, our love has nowhere to go
We found ourselves at the mercy of those whom we desired
We loved abundantly while donning suspecting hearts
We dipped our hands too often that we poisoned the well
    Soaked it dry by not setting aside enough tenderness for
    ourselves —

Watch still as untreated wounds eventually
Fester into gangrene.

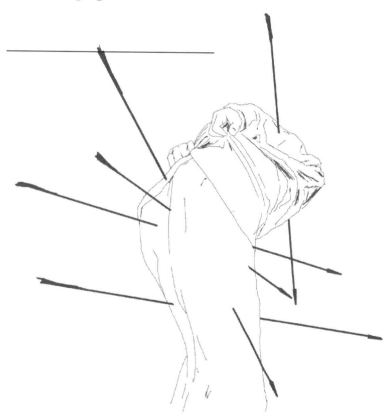

ABORTED DREAMS

My father left my mother this way –
Crow's feet resting beside her tired eyes
Calloused hands that rattled behind bars
Her greyed head pressed against the floorboard,
Desperate to hear his footsteps again
Reaching out to flashbacks and echoes
That never returned her sobs.
A hallowed vacancy refusing to be filled
The burning lamp in the basement of an old house
Fifty years of agony flew by,
She had three – maybe four – of bliss
Through rose-coloured lenses
Rolling slideshows of daydreams
Of all that could've been.

The next time I kiss death
I'll make sure to use
plenty of tongue.

———————

"-ISMs"

As a creature of habit,
Mannerisms, for me, ironically,
Are a wretched thing.
The Baudelaires sowed their visceral compulsions
Of closing storybooks
At the height of their happier chapters
To stop the tales from
Meeting their bitter endings.
Under the chokehold of predestination,
Our favourite lore came to end –
    Anachronic and absolute
There's no shame in our obsession.
Our mind became a prison,
Coddling our porcelain hearts
With reservations worn on our sleeves
And ritualism in our strut.
Disenchantment wrinkles the pages
Just like eating glass.
I must unlearn a custom
Of keeping alive vibrant stories
That have already long died.

HEAVEN FORBID

Heaven forbid,
    I forget you
        and the softness in your breath
        how it rippled across my skin
            teeming with excitement.

Heaven forbid,
    I replace you
        and the taste of a name
            quivering on my lips.

Heaven forbid,
    I long for you
        and the kiss you never gave away
            rolling off my tongue.

Heaven forbid,
    I erase you,
        Licking the wounds of
            Our incompatibilities.

No matter how quickly the glamour fades,
    Don't ever look back in regret.

———————

Keep your kingdoms
All I need is a late sunset,
A muse to love early mornings,
And a timely death.

———————

SWANSONG

Our home is losing its greatest pride
To the briefness of eternity.
Babylon fading.
Though kingdoms flit away
And temples crumble,
We are left enshrined inside museums
Tucked in the heartland of myths,
In gospels and history books ashened with idolatry
Like Autumn leaves reminisced in contentious splendour.
We made a fool of death with our art
Perpetual. Transcendental. Divine.
They shall build statues of us
On sacred leylines running down
The unforgiving coast
Venice sunsets
Eclipsing a senile, joyless land
Pontificating our art of yesterdays
For as long as tolerable.
Save your flowers, your eulogies, and alms.
Don't paint us grey
When we used to be so golden.

THE SPOTLESS MIND

At 17, I belonged to the highs and the momentary bliss
Sputtering and lumbering in a folly
A constant friend presided over me as a master.
Sweeter than heaven, temptation like sin
And I fell hard for its rare magic.
When we poured ourselves our first goodbye,
No downpours can quell the drought in my heart.
Three fingers of loose ends;
The what-ifs unspool profusely.
Ten years in and out of sobriety,
I'm still hungover from the taste of it.
Addiction on the rocks overflowing with regrets
A frothing heaviness compresses my ribs,
My thirst dances with concrete feet.
Out of the morning,
I hope to find a clearing in my mind,
A harbour in my tempest
The flood will wash away all traces of it
Its name will no longer be my disease
A sudden peace will embrace me
My lungs will be drained of all its dry water.
I will be over it in the fullness of time,
Thinking this must be what it feels like
To finally be clean.

THANKS

Thank you Jaesa for your gentle heart and open mind, for your constant encouragement and your compassion. To Mon, for your imagination and faith in my words. To Paris, for instilling in me a new love for poetry. To Ja, for being a bright spot in my life. To Maryam for teaching me the word 'tiris'. To my favourites: Sammie, Heart, Bill, Ken, mom & dad for leading me into constant adventures, for your appetite for creativity and wisdom, for ushering me out of my shell some many years ago, and never stopping since. For being the fearless embodiment of bewilderment and curiosity; thank you.

With my total love.

ABOUT THE AUTHOR

Liethers is the alter ego of a resident storyteller and illustrator from the vibrant city of Abu Dhabi. They received their Honours degree from Heriot-Watt University. 'Whiskey for The Uninitiated' is Liethers' second poetry release and first full collection. Choosing to remain anonymous, their poetry and essays have been featured under the same nom de plume in several journals, publications, and poetry anthology books. The child of a Navy veteran and an aviation alumnus, Liethers grew up cultivating life experiences on the road and credits their parents for broadening their horizons and introducing them to different cultures and landscapes early on in their formative years. This has set the pace for Liethers' nomadic identity as an uprooted foreigner belonging both everywhere and nowhere through art.

If you would like to know more about the author, get connected on social media. Liethers goes by the handle **@WeTheMythical** on Instagram and Twitter. You can also find free books and exclusive artworks on their website: www.lietherspoetry.tk

Printed in Great Britain
by Amazon

67848932R00099